# Dewey Bob

## Judy Schachner

Dial Books  for Young Readers

To Carol,
xox judy

Dial Books for Young Readers
Penguin Young Readers Group
An imprint of Penguin Random House, LLC
375 Hudson Street
New York, NY 10014

Library of Congress Cataloging-in-Publication Data
Schachner, Judith Byron, author, illustrator.
  Dewey Bob / by Judy Schachner.
      pages cm
  Summary: Dewey Bob Crockett is a young raccoon who loves to collect shiny things, but he discovers that it is a lot harder for a raccoon to collect—and keep—a friend.
  ISBN 978-0-8037-4120-1 (hardcover)
1.  Raccoon—Juvenile fiction. 2.  Friendship—Juvenile fiction. [1. Raccoon—Fiction. 2. Friendship—Fiction.]  I. Title.
  PZ7.S3286De 2015
  [E]—dc23                    2014043740

Printed in China on acid-free paper

10 9 8 7 6 5 4 3 2 1

Designed by Lily Malcom
Text set in Klepto

The illustrations for this book were created in acrylics, gouache, collage, mixed media, and the kitchen sink.

**Dewey Bob Crockett** was born in
the pocket of an old pair of pants.

And when he got too big for his britches, Dewey knew what he had to do. "Time to find yer own pair of pants, son," said Ma Crockett, wiping away a tear. "And don't forget to take yer buttons," she added, handing him one for the road.

True, Dewey had never met a button he didn't like. But when his collection began to weigh down the family pants, Dewey knew it was time to move on.

He wasn't exactly sad about leaving, because Dewey had mastered every raccoon rule there was in the book, especially the one about washing stuff. "Why, I'm as clean as the beans are green!" declared Dewey every time he spun his little paws around a bar of soap.

But finding a home that was big enough was harder than he had ever imagined. Because Dewey collected far more than just buttons. . . . He collected experiences, too. "There's only so much a heart can hold," said Dewey, opening up an old glass jar, "before it begins to overflow."

"That's one heck of a moon,"
said the raccoon with a sigh.
"And I'm gonna save me some."

Dewey had just about given up finding a place, when over
yonder he spied a LARGE pair of pants hanging on a clothesline.
For a brief moment, Dewey was tempted to move right into the
left leg and call it a night . . . but that's when he saw it!

No pants for me!
No pants for me!
'Cuz I'm gonna Live
IN a BIG oak
TREE,

he sang, looking straight
up at his future home.

The place was as empty as a hatched egg . . . and filthy, too!
But a little dirt didn't scare Dewey. "I'm a mean, clean, washin' machine!"
said the li'l raccoon as he scrubbed the place spotless. Then he took a
long soak in the tub with some of his favorite buttons.

Perhaps a stripe would be nice...

"Sweet mother of marbles, " said Dewey, looking around, "this place needs some
decoratin'!" So Dewey dried off and went out to do a little shopping.

The first stop was a row of trash cans, but they were way too crowded for his liking.

Then he moseyed on down to his favorite spot—the dump!—where
Dewey Bob fished from a mountain of lost and tossed things.

Some folks' trash is a raccoon's treasure, and Dewey Bob Crockett will pick it all for Pleasure!

When his cart was full, Dewey Bob pushed it over to a small stream and scrubbed his catch until it was as clean as a bucketful of bleached bones. Then he brought it all back home.

Dewey worked day and night separating his odds from his ends. "Now this here has potential!" he said, holding up an end. Then that li'l rascal set to work doing what Dewey did best—making things. Some things were downright practical, while other things were what Dewey called "art."

"This is a real humdinger,"
declared Dewey Bob.

But as he ran his tiny paws up and down and all around his new creation, he began to feel a case of the itchy-twitchies creeping up his spine, a sure sign that a spell of collectin' was coming on.

So Dewey grabbed a clean glass jar, stepped outside of his tree, and collected the very first things he saw—fireflies! Dewey was partial to sparkly things, but he didn't have the heart to keep them.

Truth was, Dewey had begun to miss Ma Crockett back home in the family pants. And feeling a tad bit lonesome, the little fellow did something real unusual for a nocturnal creature. He went to bed.

But before Dewey fell asleep, he needed to collect his thoughts.
The most important one he tucked under his pillow.

The next morning, that li'l rascal was racing down a country road with his rusty old cart, and he was tossing every critter too slow to get out of his way into it.

Squeezy, fleasy and don't ask me why, but collectin' new friends is as easy as pie!

shouted Dewey as he ran along.

But Dewey soon found out that *finding* friends
was much easier than keeping friends.

"Run fer yer lives!" hollered a squirrel, launching a nut at Dewey's head.
"He's got crazy ey-ey-ey-eyes!" bleated an old goat, scrambling out of the cart.

"And he's out in broad DAYLiGHT!" howled a one-eared dog,
 leaping into a bush.

Every critter bolted . . .

'ceptin' for one, a barely breathing, half-starved mud ball. But mud ball or not, it seemed that Dewey Bob Crockett had collected his very first friend. And he was proud as a panda wearing new plaid pants.

"Collectin' makes me hungry, too," declared Dewey as he strolled over to the nearest trash can.

The mud ball was not impressed.

When even the smell of a moldy old pork chop failed to get a rise out of the critter, Dewey began to wonder if his new friend was really a critter at all.

"Maybe you *is* just an old ball of mud," he said.
But then Dewey Bob leaned in and gave the thing a squeeze.

As soon as the two of them arrived back home, Dewey did what he always did with his collectibles. He gave the mud ball a darn good scrubbing.

True, Dewey could never tell the difference between a puppy and a kitten. But he always knew when something needed fixing. "No wonder you didn't run like them other critters," said Dewey, feeling his heart begin to break. "You couldn't." Then he tucked his little friend into bed, tighter than a blossom in a buttonhole.

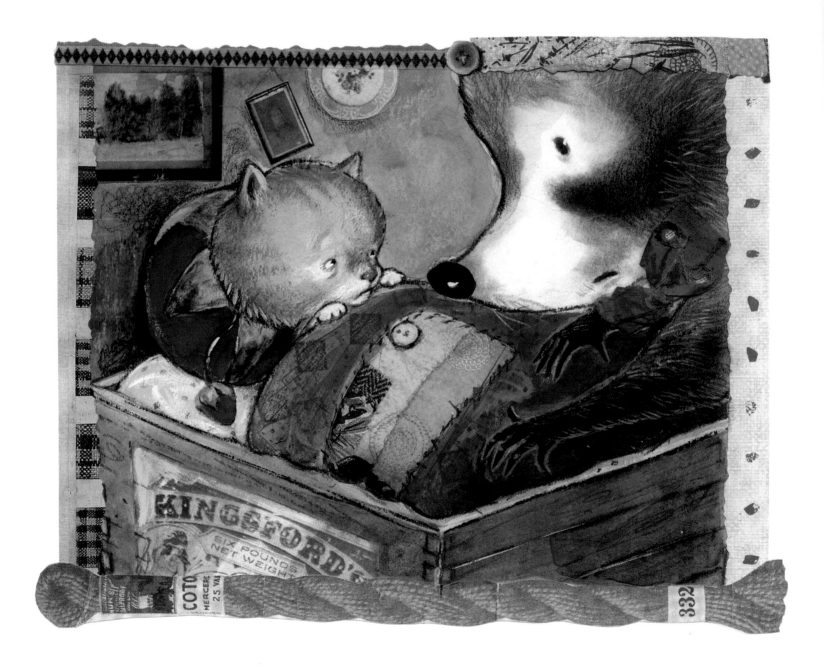

That night as the mud ball slept, Dewey Bob snuck into his workshop and took out two of his most prized possessions. Then he got right down to work.

Come sunup, Dewey had made something as practical as it was pretty out of two big buttons and a handful of odds and ends.

"Mercy!" he declared as he ran his paws up and down and all around his new creation. "If those wheels ain't as round as the rings on a raccoon's tail."

Then he waited for the mud ball to wake up.

Well, it was no surprise that the little critter took to his wheels like a bear takes to bedroom slippers.

Giddyup, Puppy.

And even though it made Dewey dizzy to watch his little friend roll around the room all day long, he couldn't remember a time when he felt happier.

Sorry about the nut, Dewey.
That's so tweet.
AMA-A-A-Zing!
Sigh...
Take it slow.
I want Pants!
I need me an ear.
Oh Homer, you're Perfect just the way you are.

But the truth is, the mud ball wasn't a thing. He was a livin', breathin' critter who deserved to experience the world in all its splendor. And Dewey knew it. So first he opened his heart . . . and then he opened the front door. "Roll on, Mudball, roll on."

And roll he did . . . right back into the arms of his very best friend.

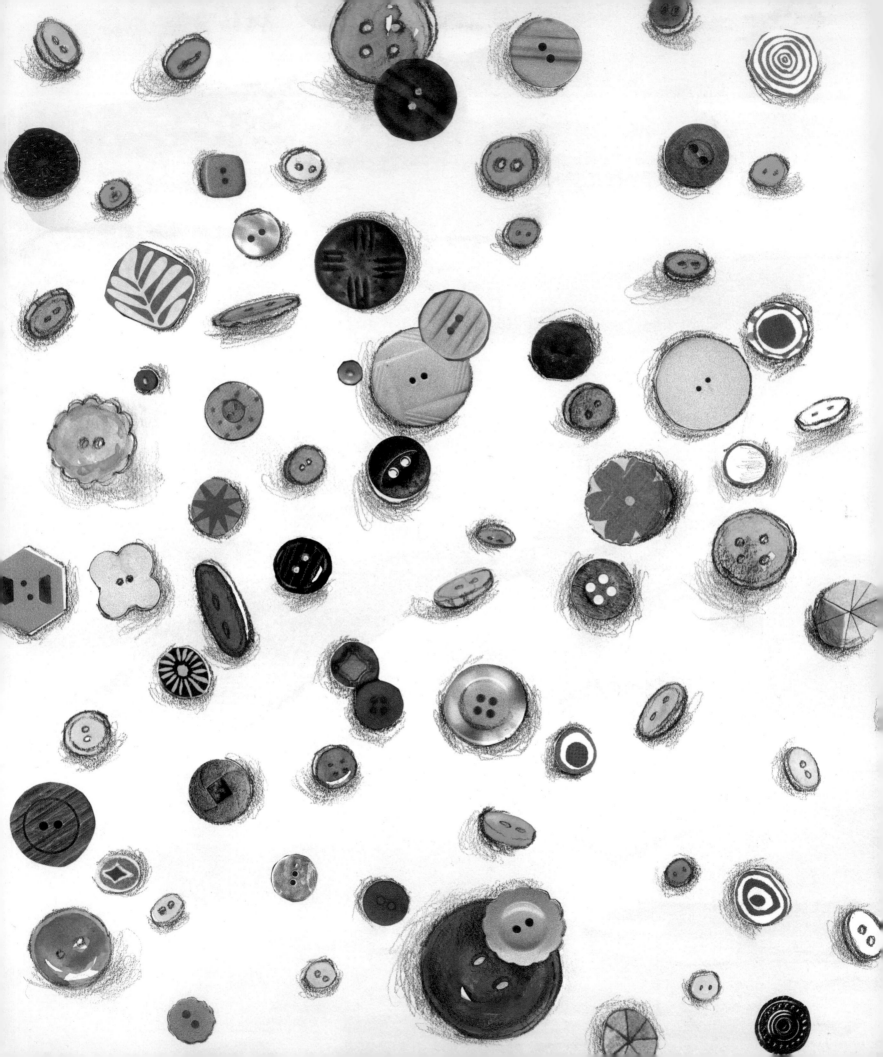